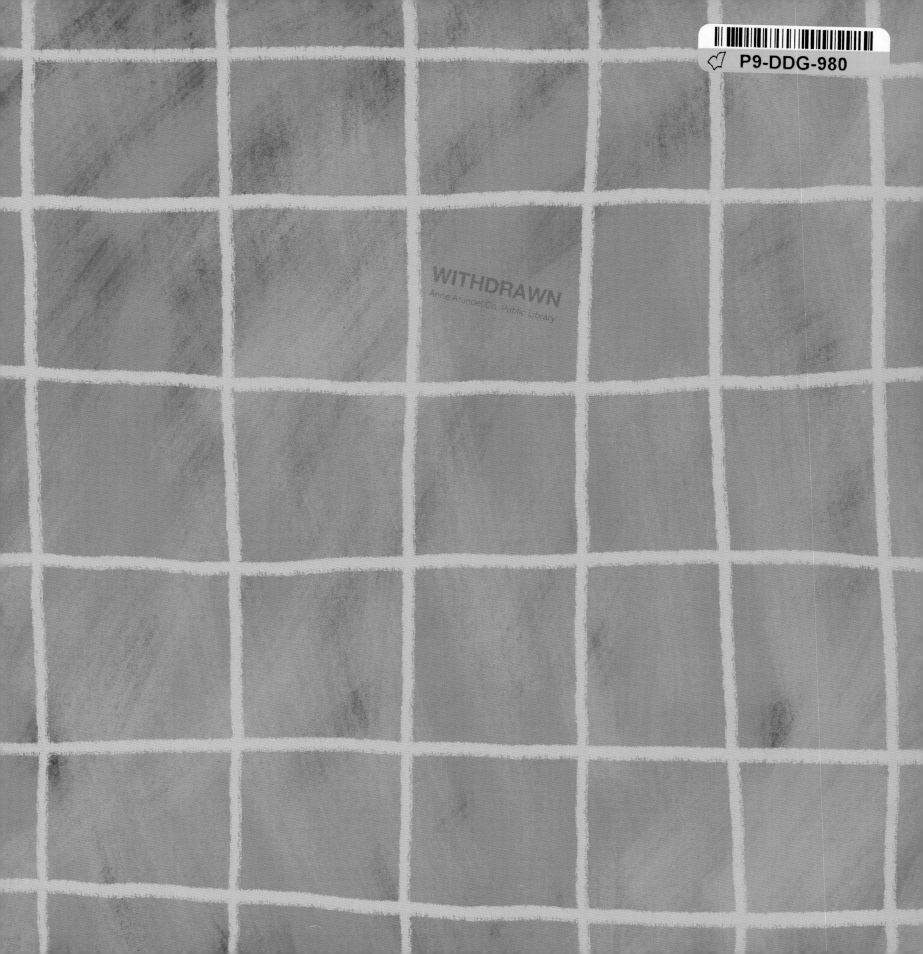

NAPTASTROPHE!

JARRETT J. KROSOCZKA

Alfred A. Knopf New York

THIS IS A BORZOI BOOK PUBLISHED BY ALFRED A. KNOPF

Copyright © 2017 by Jarrett J. Krosoczka. All rights reserved. Published in the United States by Alfred A. Knopf, an imprint of Random House Children's Books, a division of Penguin Random House LLC, New York. Knopf, Borzoi Books, and the colophon are registered trademarks of Penguin Random House LLC.
Visit us on the Web! randomhousekids.com. Educators and librarians, for a variety of teaching tools, visit us at RHTeachersLibrarians.com

Library of Congress Cataloging-in-Publication Data is available upon request.

ISBN 978-0-385-75483-5 (trade) — ISBN 978-0-385-75484-2 (lib. bdg.) — ISBN 978-0-385-75485-9 (ebook)

The text of this book is set in 25-point Supernett cn Regular.
MANUFACTURED IN CHINA   May 2017   10 9 8 7 6 5 4 3 2 1
First Edition
Random House Children's Books supports the First Amendment and celebrates the right to read.

For my sweet Lucy,
whose refusal to nap inspired this book

It seemed that nobody listened to Lucy
when she said, "I'm not tired."

So she found herself in her room.
With the lights off.
During the daytime.

There must have been a mistake.
She yelled,

"I'm not tired!"

But . . . nothing.

Lucy thought of all the fun she was missing.

She could be playing with her toys.

Her toys probably missed her.

But what if they didn't?

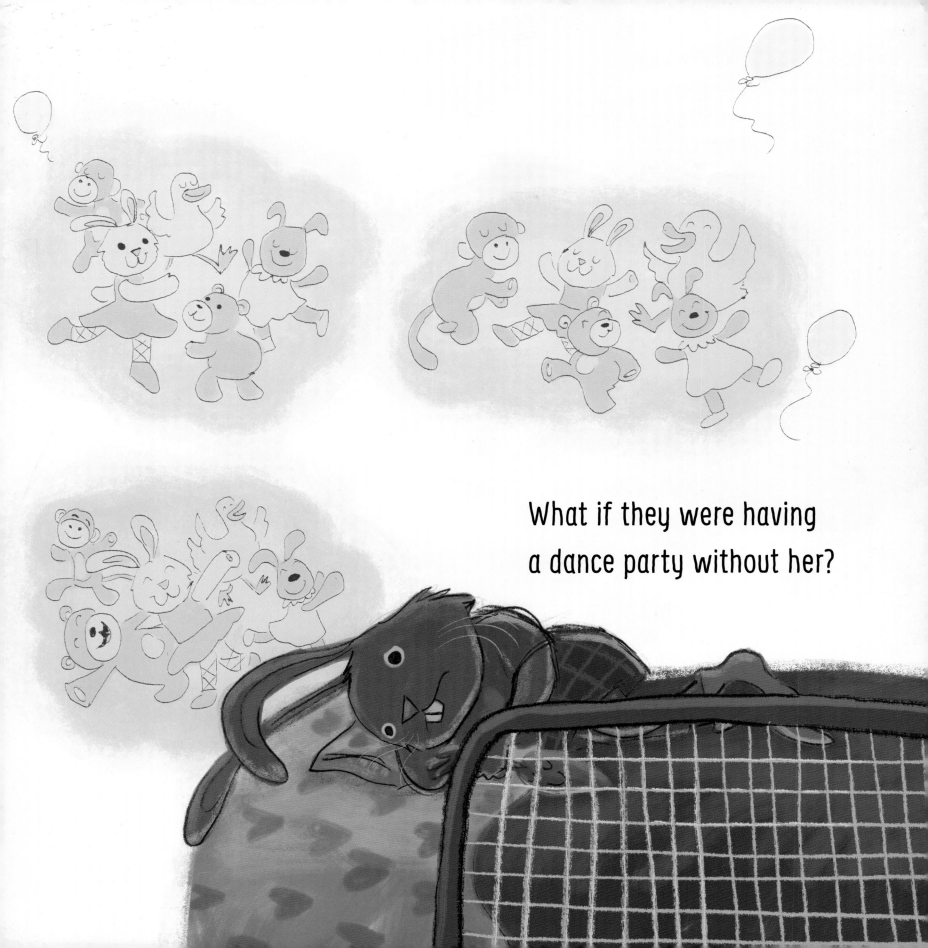

What if they were having
a dance party without her?

After an eternity, Lucy's bedroom door opened.

"I'm not tiiiiired!"
she said proudly.

She hadn't slept. But now it was too late for naptime— she and her daddy needed to run errands.

Lucy called her daddy on a banana. **"Not tired,"** she said, but he didn't answer his phone.

"Still not tired!" Lucy shouted moments later.

"Not tired."   "Not tired."

"Not tired,
not tired,
not tired."

"Look!" exclaimed Lucy. "Candy!"
"We're not getting candy today, sweetheart,"
said her daddy.

"We'll just get a few," said Lucy.

"I said no," her daddy reminded her.

And then it hit her.

The lights. The noise.

Her knees wobbled.

Her eyes drooped.

Lucy could not
hold it in any longer.

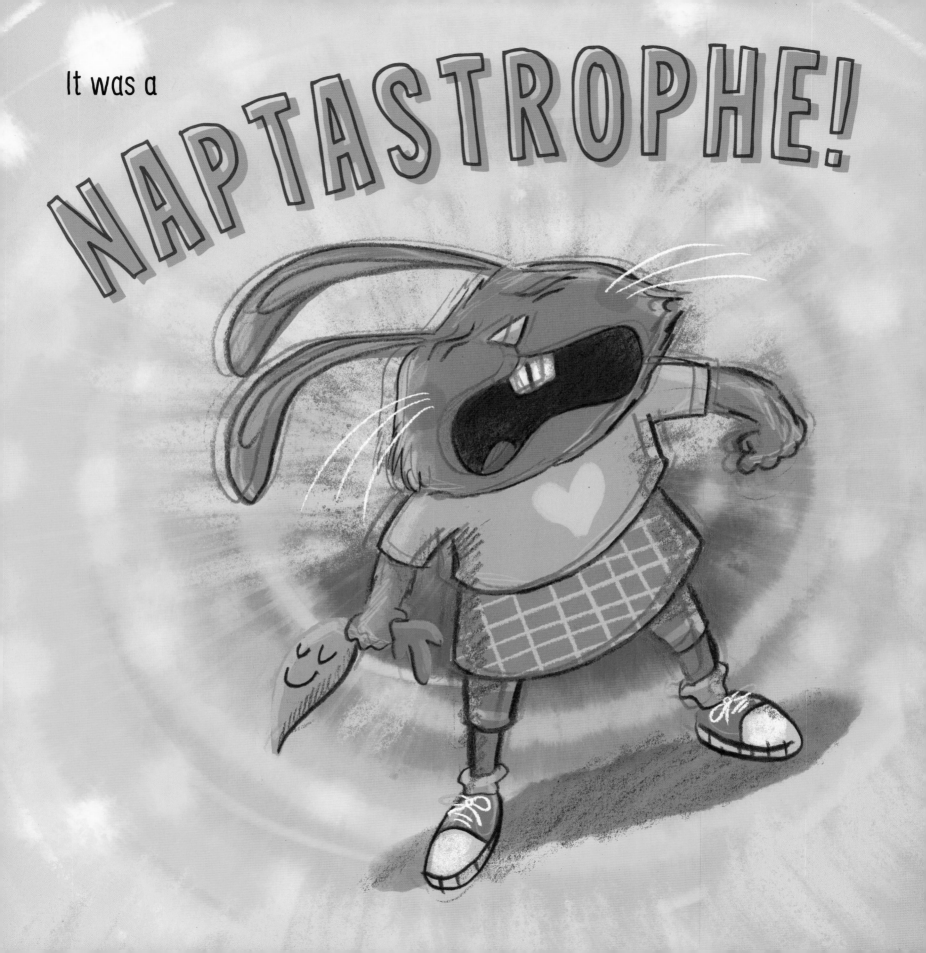

Her arms flapped.

Her fists locked.

She got stuck to the floor.

It was time to go.

At dinner, Lucy heard the word "bedtime."

She interrupted the grown-up talk to say,
"I'M NOT TIIIIIIIRED!"

Just before . . .

Good night, Lucy.

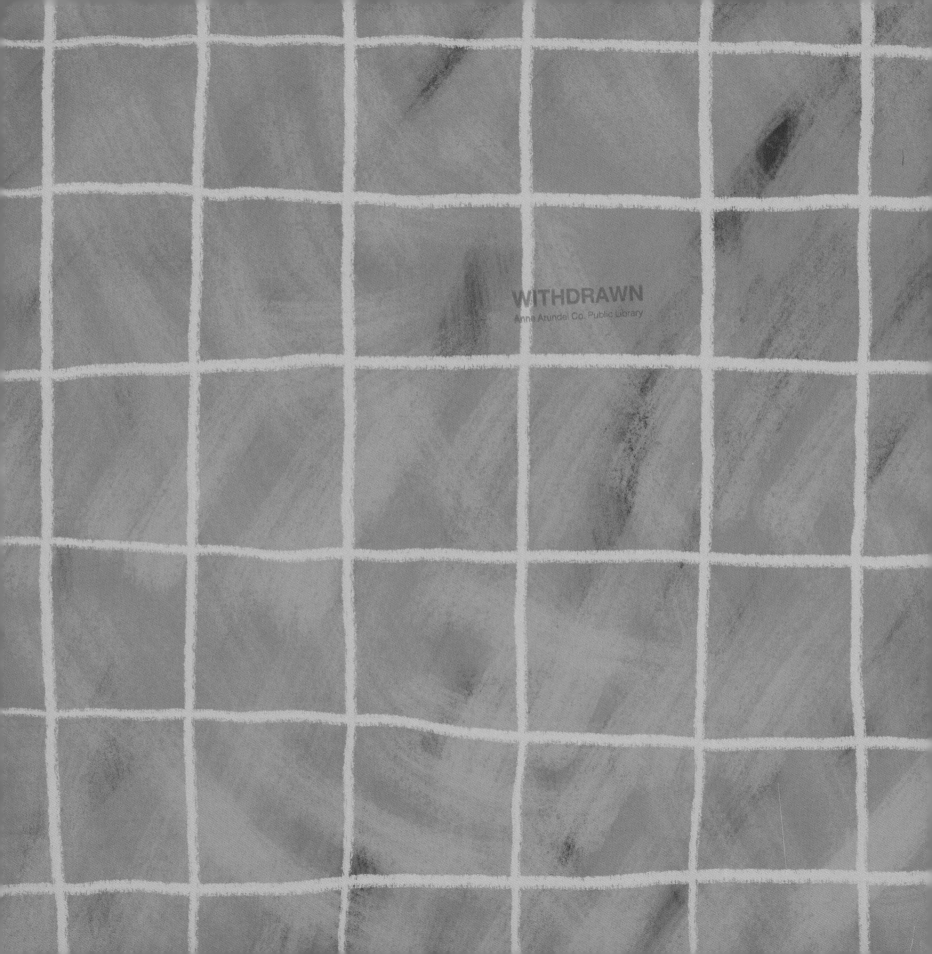